By Luisa McLaurin

SNEAK PEEK
FASHIONS AND ME

Illustrated by Hameo

© 2022 Luisa McLaurin

All rights reserved. No part of this publication may be reproduced, distributed, or transmitted in any form or by any means, including photocopying, recording, or other electronic or mechanical methods, without the prior written permission of the publisher, except in the case of brief quotations embodied in critical reviews and certain other noncommercial uses permitted by copyright law.

ISBN: 978-1-66784-607-1

DEDICATIONS

To all my children, James, Quincy, Ryon
And a Special Thanks
To my daughter Tanisha Ferguson as she helped
Complete City's last name Garland and for
Being my biggest supporter and sponsor

To the Awesome Three
My granddaughters Kayden Denise and Riley
And to my great niece Bailey
Which the main characters are inspired by

To Ha Meo
My brilliant illustrator
For making my vision come to life in a way
That I could only dream.

And a final thank you to
Amanda Toolanen
Who continually inspires

My inspiration
To all Children around the world
DREAM BIG!

Let me introduce myself. My name is City-City Garland. I am now eight years old, and I live with my mom and dad in New York City. My dad is in the military and often away fighting for our country and helping millions of people around the world, which is why he's my hero. And my mom, she's just amazing and my inspiration. She's a seamstress, just like my two aunts and grandmother. What's a seamstress, you ask? A seamstress is a person who sews clothes. My mom, aunts, and grandmother are business partners, run their own company, and make beautiful clothes for all sorts of people.

I want to design the clothes that my family sews. I am going to be a fashion designer! I started sketching my own line of clothing when I was just five years old. I am now ready and excited to present my collection to my mom, hoping she will agree to help me with the production of my clothing line. I am ready to be a young entrepreneur in the career I have chosen for myself. Here is my story. Are you ready for a sneak peek? Let's go!

"Good morning, City," Mom said.

"Good morning, Mom," I answered.

"I made you breakfast and fixed your lunch."

"Thanks, Mom."

"My, you look very pretty this morning. What's the special occasion?" Mom asked, intrigued.

"Nothing special. I decided to adjust my wardrobe by mixing and matching things in my closet."

"Your wardrobe? I like the idea," Mom says as she chuckled.

"Thank you." I smiled as I start off to school. "Bye, Mom!"

"Bye City, have a wonderful day at school."

Just getting to school, I saw the girls, "Hi, Bailee! Hi, Kayden Denise! Hi, Riley!" I shouted. These are my cousins, we all go to the same school, and we're best friends.

Her cousin yells, "Hi City! So, have you been sketching more glamorous designs?" asked Riley.

"Yes…" I now have a collection of different designs for different occasions. I think you guys will really like them." I told the girls. The bell began to ring. "See you all at lunch," I say to my cousins. "See you at lunch," the girls yelled out as they ran off to class.

At lunch City, Kayden Denise and Riley are sitting at the lunch table when Bailee comes in, "Hey Bailee, over here!" City waved

"Hi City. Hi Kayden Denise. Hi Riley," Bailee yelled.

"City was just sharing some of her design ideas," Kayden Denise said.

"Yes, it sounds awesome," Riley replied.

"I can just imagine how amazing they will look since her mom is a seamstress," Bailee responded.

Reaching over to get some of Kayden Denise's chips. Kayden Denise tapped her hand. "Ask, Bailee," Kayden Denise said.

"Ok," Bailee responded.

"Well, City, are you going to show us at least one of your designs?" Bailee asked.

"Nope," I answered. "I want it to be a surprise to you all, just as it's going to be a big surprise to my mom."

"Ok," Bailee said.

"We can wait. Besides, I want to see the entire show," Kayden Denise said.

"That's cool," said Bailee. "Lunch is over, got to go, see you all after school."

The bell rang, and school was finally out.

"Are you ready, City?" her cousins shout simultaneously.

"Yes," I replied. "And I have all of you wearing some of my designs."

"You do?" they all replied, surprised.

"Yes. I did not want to tell you until school was out. It was a little surprise."

"Little?!" Riley said. They all laughed.

"Ok, wish me success."

"Much success!" they all yelled back.

Sara and Minchi are City's classmates, "Hey City," Sara says.

"Hey, Sara, hey Minchi."

"Hi, City," Minchi whispered softly.

"What are you four up to?" Sara asked.

"Why do you think we're up to something?" I replied.

"Well, you all looked like there is this big secret," Sara said.

"Secret?" I answered with a giggle, avoiding the question. "I don't want to miss the bus. Talk to you on Monday."

"City!" Sara yelled

"See you on Monday!" I yelled back.

Sara stands with a frown on her face as Minchi giggled.

"Mom, I'm home," I said as I changed my clothes.

"Hey City, Are you hungry? I can make you a snack."

"No, Mom it's Ok. I don't want a snack."

"You look excited about something. Would you like to share?"

"Yes, I want to share a project that I have been working on."

"Ok, do you want to tell me what this big project is?"

"Ok. You, my aunties, and grandma are all seamstresses. Your work is amazing. I have watched all of you over the years making amazing clothes which inspired me to design my own clothing line."

"Your own clothing line?" her mom said, surprised and excited.

"Yes, Mom."

"I did not know you were interested in design."

"I wanted to keep it a secret until I had designs to show you," I replied excitingly.

"Ok! Let's see them, City," Mom giggled. I sat next to my mom and opened my portfolio of designs.

"Mom, you always said that you would be the one who would take me to my fifth-grade graduation."

"Yes, and I intend to do just that, City."

"Mom, these are the dresses I designed and I would like for us to wear them to my graduation." Mom was so excited. Her eyes filled with tears of joy. She jumped up and hugged me tight.

All she could say softly under her breath was, "Beautiful, beautiful, just beautiful."

"I will!" Mom said.

"You will!" I said, smiling with glee, feeling amazingly proud. My eyes sparkled with joy.

"Yes, yes!" Mom said. She was indeed breathless as the tears rolled down her face. "Amazing, just amazing, City-City Garland."

Book II coming soon!

Download Coloring Pages of City's Fashion Designs

@

www.fashionsandme.com